Praise for The Miraculous Journey of Edward Tulane

A *New York Times Book Review* Notable Book of the Year

꙳

A Parents' Choice Gold Award Winner

꙳

"[DiCamillo] is a refreshingly graceful storyteller with a finely tuned ear for the discerning detail. . . . One reading is hardly enough."
　　　　　　　　　　　　　　　　—*The New York Times Book Review*

"Edward deserves to share space on the classics shelf. . . . Riveting, thanks to masterful storytelling and beautiful writing."
　　　　　　　　　　　　　　　　—*Cleveland Plain Dealer*

"Begs to be read again and again."　　　　　　—*Boston Globe*

"Bagram Ibatoulline's exquisite illustrations cast a warm light across this . . . tale by one of today's most admired writers for children."
　　　　　　　　　　　　　　　　—*The Wall Street Journal*

"A smooth, old-fashioned, thoughtful story. . . . Perfect."
　　　　　　　　　　　　　　　　—*Chicago Sun-Times*

"DiCamillo has a style that makes even the most mundane sentences flavorful."　　　　　　　　—*Philadelphia Inquirer*

"A remarkable, eloquent, and genuinely moving story."
　　　　　　　　　　　　　　　　—*Denver Post*

"A rare and beautiful book that remains in the soul, clear and hopeful like a bell on a cold night."　　　—*San Diego Union-Tribune*

NOVELS BY KATE DiCAMILLO

The

Miraculous Journey

of

Edward Tulane

The Miraculous Journey of

EDWARD TULANE

KATE DICAMILLO

ILLUSTRATED BY BAGRAM IBATOULLINE

CANDLEWICK PRESS

For Jane Resh Thomas,

who gave me the rabbit and told me his name

Text copyright © 2006 by Kate DiCamillo
Illustrations copyright © 2006 by Bagram Ibatoulline

"The Testing-Tree" copyright © 1968 by Stanley Kunitz, from *The Collected Poems*
by Stanley Kunitz. Used by permission of W. W. Norton & Company, Inc.

First paperback edition in this format 2015

The Library of Congress has cataloged the hardcover edition as follows:

DiCamillo, Kate.
The miraculous journey of Edward Tulane / Kate DiCamillo ;
illustrated by Bagram Ibatoulline. — 1st ed.
p.   cm.
Summary: Edward Tulane, a cold-hearted and proud toy rabbit, loves only himself
until he is separated from the little girl who adores him and travels across the country,
acquiring new owners and listening to their hopes, dreams, and histories.
ISBN 978-0-7636-2589-4 (hardcover)
[1. Toys — Fiction. 2. Rabbits — Fiction. 3. Love — Fiction. 4. Listening — Fiction.
5. Adventure and adventurers — Fiction.]   I. Ibatoulline, Bagram, ill. II. Title.
PZ7.D5455Mi 2006
[Fic] — dc22   2004056129

ISBN 978-0-7636-3987-7 (paperback)
ISBN 978-0-7636-4367-6 (reformatted paperback)
ISBN 978-0-7636-8090-9 (second reformatted paperback)

22 23 24 TRC 25 24 23 22 21

Printed in Eagan, MN, U.S.A.

This book was typeset in CentaurMT.
The illustrations were done in acrylic gouache.

Candlewick Press
99 Dover Street
Somerville, Massachusetts 02144

visit us at www.candlewick.com

The heart breaks and breaks
and lives by breaking.
It is necessary to go
through dark and deeper dark
and not to turn.

— from "The Testing-Tree," by Stanley Kunitz

CHAPTER ONE

ONCE, IN A HOUSE ON EGYPT STREET, there lived a rabbit who was made almost entirely of china. He had china arms and china legs, china paws and a china head, a china torso and a china nose. His arms and legs were jointed and joined by wire so that his china elbows and china knees could be bent, giving him much freedom of movement.

His ears were made of real rabbit fur, and beneath the fur, there were strong, bendable wires, which allowed the ears to be arranged into poses that reflected the rabbit's mood—jaunty, tired, full of ennui. His tail, too, was made of real rabbit fur and was fluffy and soft and well shaped.

The rabbit's name was Edward Tulane, and he was tall. He measured almost three feet from the tip of his ears to the tip of his feet; his eyes were painted a penetrating and intelligent blue.

In all, Edward Tulane felt himself to be an exceptional specimen. Only his whiskers gave him pause. They were long and elegant (as they should be), but they were of uncertain origin. Edward felt quite strongly that they were not the whiskers of a rabbit. Whom the whiskers had belonged to initially—what unsavory animal—was a question that Edward could not bear to consider for too long. And so he did not. He preferred, as a rule, not to think unpleasant thoughts.

Edward's mistress was a ten-year-old, dark-haired girl named Abilene Tulane, who thought almost as highly of Edward as Edward thought of himself. Each morning after she dressed herself for school, Abilene dressed Edward.

The china rabbit was in possession of an

extraordinary wardrobe composed of handmade silk suits, custom shoes fashioned from the finest leather and designed specifically for his rabbit feet, and a wide array of hats equipped with holes so that they could easily fit over Edward's large and expressive ears. Each pair of well-cut pants had a small pocket for Edward's gold pocket watch. Abilene wound this watch for him each morning.

"Now, Edward," she said to him after she was done winding the watch, "when the big hand is on the twelve and the little hand is on the three, I will come home to you."

She placed Edward on a chair in the dining room and positioned the chair so that Edward was looking out the window and could see the path that led up to the Tulane front door. Abilene balanced the watch on his left leg. She kissed the tips of his ears, and then she left and Edward spent the day staring out at Egypt Street, listening to the tick of his watch and waiting.

Of all the seasons of the year, the rabbit most preferred winter, for the sun set early then and the dining-room windows became dark and Edward could see his own reflection in the glass. And what a reflection it was! What an elegant figure he cut! Edward never ceased to be amazed at his own fineness.

In the evening, Edward sat at the dining-room table with the other members of the Tulane family: Abilene; her mother and father; and Abilene's grandmother, who was called Pellegrina. True, Edward's ears barely cleared the tabletop, and true also, he spent the duration of the meal staring straight ahead at nothing but the bright and blinding white of the tablecloth. But he was there, a rabbit at the table.

Abilene's parents found it charming that Abilene considered Edward real, and that she sometimes requested that a phrase or story be repeated because Edward had not heard it.

"Papa," Abilene would say, "I'm afraid that Edward didn't catch that last bit."

Abilene's father would then turn in the direction of Edward's ears and speak slowly, repeating what he had just said for the benefit of the china rabbit. Edward pretended, out of courtesy to Abilene, to listen. But, in truth, he was not very interested in what people had to say. And also, he did not care for Abilene's parents and their condescending manner toward him. All adults, in fact, condescended to him.

Only Abilene's grandmother spoke to him as Abilene did, as one equal to another. Pellegrina was very old. She had a large, sharp nose and bright, black eyes that shone like dark stars. It was Pellegrina who was responsible for Edward's existence. It was she who had commissioned his making, she who had ordered his silk suits and his pocket watch, his jaunty hats and his bendable ears, his fine leather shoes and his jointed arms and legs, all from a master craftsman in her native France. It was Pellegrina who had given him as a gift to Abilene on her seventh birthday.

And it was Pellegrina who came each night to tuck Abilene into her bed and Edward into his.

"Will you tell us a story, Pellegrina?" Abilene asked her grandmother each night.

"Not tonight, lady," said Pellegrina.

"When?" asked Abilene. "What night?"

"Soon," said Pellegrina. "Soon there will be a story."

And then she turned off the light, and Edward and Abilene lay in the dark of the bedroom.

"I love you, Edward," Abilene said each night after Pellegrina had left. She said those words and then she waited, almost as if she expected Edward to say something in return.

Edward said nothing. He said nothing because, of course, he could not speak. He lay in his small bed next to Abilene's large one. He stared up at the ceiling and listened to the sound of her breath entering and leaving her body, knowing that soon she would be asleep. Because Edward's eyes were painted on and he could not close them, he was always awake.

Sometimes, if Abilene put him into his bed on his side instead of on his back, he could see through the cracks in the curtains and out into the dark night. On clear nights, the stars shone, and their pinprick light comforted Edward in a way that he could not quite understand. Often, he stared at the stars all night until the dark finally gave way to dawn.

CHAPTER TWO

AND IN THIS MANNER, EDWARD'S days passed, one into the other. Nothing remarkable happened. Oh, there was the occasional small, domestic drama. Once, while Abilene was at school, the neighbor's dog, a male brindled boxer inexplicably named Rosie, came into the house uninvited and unannounced and lifted his leg on the dining-room table, spraying the white tablecloth with urine. He then trotted over and sniffed Edward, and before Edward even had time to consider the implications of being sniffed by a dog, he was in Rosie's mouth and Rosie was shaking him back and forth vigorously, growling and drooling.

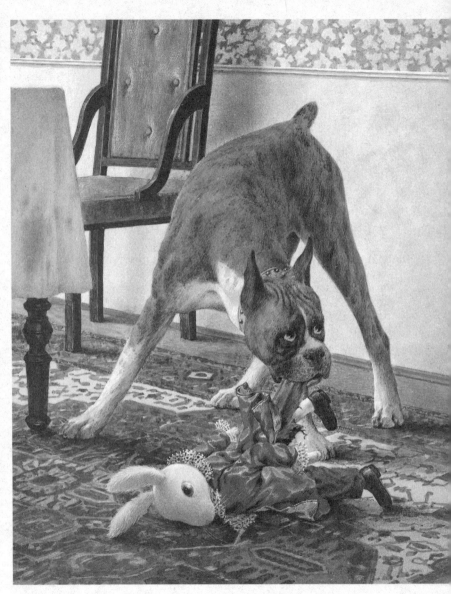

"Drop it!" she shouted to Rosie.

Fortunately, Abilene's mother walked past the dining room and witnessed Edward's suffering.

"Drop it!" she shouted to Rosie.

And Rosie, surprised into obedience, did as he was told.

Edward's silk suit was stained with drool and his head ached for several days afterward, but it was his ego that had suffered the most damage. Abilene's mother had referred to him as "it," and she was more outraged at the dog urine on her tablecloth than she was about the indignities that Edward had suffered at the jaws of Rosie.

And then there was the time that a maid, new to the Tulane household and eager to impress her employers with her diligence, came upon Edward sitting on his chair in the dining room.

"What's this bunny doing here?" she said out loud.

Edward did not care at all for the word *bunny*. He found it derogatory in the extreme.

The maid bent over him and looked into his eyes.

"Hmph," she said. She stood back up. She put her hands on her hips. "I reckon you're just like every other thing in this house, something needing to be cleaned and dusted."

And so the maid vacuumed Edward Tulane. She sucked each of his long ears up the vacuum-cleaner hose. She pawed at his clothes and beat his tail. She dusted his face with brutality and efficiency. And in her zeal to clean him, she vacuumed Edward's gold pocket watch right off his lap. The watch went into the maw of the vacuum cleaner with a distressing *clank* that the maid did not even seem to hear.

When she was done, she put the dining-room chair back at the table, and uncertain about exactly where Edward belonged, she finally decided to shove him in among the dolls on a shelf in Abilene's bedroom.

"That's right," said the maid. "There you go."

She left Edward on the shelf at a most awkward and inhuman angle—his nose was actually touching his knees; and he waited there, with the dolls twittering and giggling at him like a flock of demented and unfriendly birds, until Abilene came home from school and found him missing and ran from room to room calling his name.

"Edward!" she shouted. "Edward!"

There was no way, of course, for him to let her know where he was, no way for him to answer her. He could only sit and wait.

When Abilene found him, she held him close, so close that Edward could feel her heart beating, leaping almost out of her chest in its agitation.

"Edward," she said, "oh, Edward. I love you. I never want you to be away from me."

The rabbit, too, was experiencing a great emotion. But it was not love. It was annoyance that he had been so mightily inconvenienced, that he had been handled by the maid as cavalierly as an inanimate object—a serving bowl, say, or a teapot. The only satisfaction to be had from the whole affair was that the new maid was dismissed immediately.

Edward's pocket watch was located later, deep within the bowels of the vacuum cleaner, dented, but still in working condition; it was returned to him by Abilene's father, who presented it with a mocking bow.

"Sir Edward," he said. "Your timepiece, I believe?"

The Rosie Affair and the Vacuum-Cleaner Incident—those were the great dramas of Edward's life until the night of Abilene's eleventh birthday when, at the dinner table, as the cake was being served, the ship was mentioned.

CHAPTER THREE

SHE IS CALLED THE *QUEEN MARY,*" said Abilene's father, "and you and your mama and I shall sail on her all the way to London."

"What about Pellegrina?" said Abilene.

"I will not go," said Pellegrina. "I will stay."

Edward, of course, was not listening. He found the talk around the dinner table excruciatingly dull; in fact, he made a point of *not* listening if he could help it. But then Abilene did something unusual, something that forced him to pay attention. As the talk about the ship continued, Abilene reached for Edward and took him from his chair and stood him in her lap.

"And what about Edward?" she said, her voice high and uncertain.

"What about him, darling?" said her mother.

"Will Edward be sailing on the *Queen Mary* with us?"

"Well, of course, if you wish, although you are getting a little old for such things as china rabbits."

"Nonsense," said Abilene's father jovially. "Who would protect Abilene if Edward was not there?"

From the vantage point of Abilene's lap, Edward could see the whole table spread out before him in a way that he never could when he was seated in his own chair. He looked upon the glittering array of silverware and glasses and plates. He saw the amused and condescending looks of Abilene's parents. And then his eyes met Pellegrina's.

She was looking at him in the way a hawk hanging lazily in the air might study a mouse on the ground. Perhaps the rabbit fur on Edward's ears and tail, and the whiskers on his nose had some dim memory of being hunted, for a shiver went through him.

"Yes," said Pellegrina without taking her eyes off Edward, "who would watch over Abilene if the rabbit were not there?"

That night, when Abilene asked, as she did every night, if there would be a story, Pellegrina said, "Tonight, lady, there will be a story."

Abilene sat up in bed. "I think that Edward needs to sit here with me," she said, "so that he can hear the story, too."

"I think that is best," said Pellegrina. "Yes, I think that the rabbit must hear the story."

Abilene picked Edward up, sat him next to her in bed, and arranged the covers around him; then she said to Pellegrina, "We are ready now."

"So," said Pellegrina. She coughed. "And so. The story begins with a princess."

"A beautiful princess?" Abilene asked.

"A very beautiful princess."

"How beautiful?"

"You must listen," said Pellegrina. "It is all in the story."

CHAPTER FOUR

ONCE THERE WAS A PRINCESS WHO
was very beautiful. She shone as bright as the stars
on a moonless night. But what difference did it
make that she was beautiful? None. No difference."

"Why did it make no difference?" asked
Abilene.

"Because," said Pellegrina, "she was a princess
who loved no one and cared nothing for love, even
though there were many who loved her."

At this point in her story, Pellegrina stopped
and looked right at Edward. She stared deep into
his painted-on eyes, and again, Edward felt a shiver
go through him.

"BECAUSE," SAID PELLEGRINA, "SHE WAS A PRINCESS WHO LOVED NO ONE AND CARED NOTHING FOR LOVE, EVEN THOUGH THERE WERE MANY WHO LOVED HER."

"And so," said Pellegrina, still staring at Edward.

"What happened to the princess?" said Abilene.

"And so," said Pellegrina, turning back to Abilene, "the king, her father, said that the princess must marry; and soon after this, a prince came from a neighboring kingdom and he saw the princess and, immediately, he loved her. He gave her a ring of pure gold. He placed it on her finger. He said these words to her: 'I love you.' But do you know what the princess did?"

Abilene shook her head.

"She swallowed the ring. She took it from her finger and swallowed it. She said, 'That is what I think of love.' And she ran from the prince. She left the castle and went deep into the woods. And so."

"And so what?" said Abilene. "What happened then?"

"And so, the princess became lost in the woods.

She wandered for many days. Finally, she came to a little hut, and she knocked on the door. She said, 'Let me in; I am cold.'

"There was no answer.

"She knocked again. She said, 'Let me in; I am hungry.'

"A terrible voice answered her. The voice said, 'Enter if you must.'

"The beautiful princess entered, and she saw a witch sitting at a table counting pieces of gold.

"'Three thousand six hundred and twenty-two,' said the witch.

"'I am lost,' said the beautiful princess.

"'What of it?' said the witch. 'Three thousand six hundred and twenty-three.'

"'I am hungry,' said the princess.

"'Not my concern,' said the witch. 'Three thousand six hundred and twenty-four.'

"'But I am a beautiful princess,' said the princess.

"'Three thousand six hundred and twenty-five,' replied the witch.

"'My father,' said the princess, 'is a powerful king. You must help me or there will be consequences.'

"'Consequences?' said the witch. She looked up from her gold. She stared at the princess. 'You dare to talk to me of consequences? Very well, then, we will speak of consequences: tell me the name of the one you love.'

"'Love!' said the princess. She stamped her foot. 'Why must everyone always speak of love?'

"'Whom do you love?' said the witch. 'You must tell me the name.'

"'I love no one,' said the princess proudly.

"'You disappoint me,' said the witch. She raised her hand and said one word: 'Farthfigery.'

"And the beautiful princess was changed into a warthog.

"'What have you done to me?' squealed the princess.

"'Talk to me of consequences now, will you?' said the witch, and she went back to counting her pieces of gold. 'Three thousand six hundred and twenty-six,' said the witch as the warthog princess ran from the hut and out again into the forest.

"The kings' men were in the forest, too. And what were they looking for? A beautiful princess. And so when they came upon an ugly warthog, they shot it immediately. Pow!"

"No," said Abilene.

"Yes," said Pellegrina. "The men took the warthog back to the castle and the cook slit open its belly and inside it she found a ring of pure gold. There were many hungry people in the castle that night and all of them were waiting to be fed. So the cook put the ring on her finger and finished butchering the warthog. And the ring that the beautiful princess had swallowed shone on the cook's hand as she did her work. The end."

"The end?" said Abilene indignantly.

"Yes," said Pellegrina, "the end."

"But it can't be."

"Why can't it be?"

"Because it came too quickly. Because no one is living happily ever after, that's why."

"Ah, and so." Pellegrina nodded. She was quiet for a moment. "But answer me this: how can a story end happily if there is no love? But. Well. It is late. And you must go to sleep."

Pellegrina took Edward from Abilene. She put him in his bed and pulled the sheet up to his whiskers. She leaned close to him. She whispered, "You disappoint me."

After the old lady left, Edward lay in his small bed and stared up at the ceiling. The story, he thought, had been pointless. But then most stories were. He thought of the princess and how she had become a warthog. How gruesome! How grotesque! What a terrible fate!

"Edward," said Abilene, "I love you. I don't care how old I get, I will always love you."

Yes, yes, thought Edward.

He continued to stare up at the ceiling. He was agitated for some reason that he could not name. He wished that Pellegrina had put him on his side so that he might look at the stars.

And then he remembered Pellegrina's description of the beautiful princess. She shone as bright as the stars on a moonless night. For some reason, Edward found comfort in these words and he repeated them to himself—*as bright as the stars on a moonless night, as bright as the stars on a moonless night*—over and over until, at last, the first light of dawn appeared.

CHAPTER FIVE

THE HOUSE ON EGYPT STREET became frantic with activity as the Tulane family prepared for their voyage to England. Edward possessed a small trunk, and Abilene packed it for him, filling it with his finest suits and several of his best hats and three pairs of shoes, all so that he might cut a fine figure in London. Before she placed each outfit in the trunk, she displayed it to him.

"Do you like this shirt with this suit?" she asked him.

Or, "Would you like to wear your black derby? You look very handsome in it. Shall we pack it?"

And then, finally, on a bright Saturday morning in May, Edward and Abilene and Mr. and Mrs. Tulane were all onboard the ship, standing at the railing. Pellegrina was at the dock. On her head, she wore a floppy hat strung around with flowers. She stared straight at Edward. Her dark eyes glowed.

"Goodbye," Abilene shouted to her grandmother. "I love you."

The ship pulled away from the dock. Pellegrina waved to Abilene.

"Goodbye, lady," she called, "goodbye."

Edward felt something damp in his ears. Abilene's tears, he supposed. He wished that she would not hold him so tight. To be clutched so fiercely often resulted in wrinkled clothing. Finally, all the people on land, including Pellegrina, disappeared. Edward, for one, was relieved to see the last of her.

As was to be expected, Edward Tulane exacted much attention onboard the ship.

"What a singular rabbit," said an elderly lady with three strings of pearls wrapped around her neck. She bent down to look more closely at Edward.

"Thank you," said Abilene.

Several little girls onboard gave Edward deep glances full of longing. They asked Abilene if they might hold him.

"No," said Abilene, "I'm afraid that he's not the kind of rabbit who likes to be held by strangers."

Two young boys, brothers named Martin and Amos, took a particular interest in Edward.

"What does he do?" Martin asked Abilene on their second day at sea. He pointed at Edward who was sitting on a deck chair with his long legs stretched in front of him.

"He doesn't do anything," said Abilene.

"Does he wind up somewhere?" asked Amos.

"No," said Abilene, "he does not wind up."

"What's the point of him then?" said Martin.

"The point is that he is Edward," said Abilene.

"That's not much of a point," said Amos.

"It's not," agreed Martin. And then, after a long thoughtful pause, he said, "I wouldn't let anybody dress me like that."

"Me neither," said Amos.

"Do his clothes come off?" asked Martin.

"Of course they do," said Abilene. "He has many different outfits. And he has his own pajamas, too. They are made of silk."

Edward, as usual, was disregarding the conversation. A breeze was blowing in off the sea, and the silk scarf wrapped around his neck billowed out behind him. On his head, he wore a straw boater. The rabbit was thinking that he must look quite dashing.

It came as a total surprise to him when he was grabbed off the deck chair and first his scarf, and then his jacket and pants, were ripped from his body. He heard his pocket watch hit the deck of the ship; and then, held upside down, he watched the watch roll merrily toward Abilene's feet.

"Look at him," said Martin. "He's even got underwear." He held Edward aloft so that Amos could see.

"Take it off," shouted Amos.

"NO!!!!" screamed Abilene.

Martin removed Edward's underwear.

Edward was paying attention now. He was mortified. He was completely naked except for the hat on his head, and the other passengers onboard the ship were looking at him, directing curious and embarrassed glances his way.

"Give him to me," screamed Abilene. "He's mine."

"No," said Amos to Martin, "give him to *me*." He clapped his hands together and then held them open. "Toss him," he said.

"Please," cried Abilene. "Don't throw him. He's made of china. He'll break."

Martin threw Edward.

And Edward sailed naked through the air. Only a moment ago, the rabbit had thought that being naked in front of a shipload of strangers was the worst thing that could happen to him. But he was wrong. It was much worse being tossed, in the same naked state, from the hands of one grubby, laughing boy to another.

Amos caught Edward and held him up, displaying him triumphantly.

"Throw him back," called Martin.

Amos raised his arm, but just as he was getting ready to throw Edward, Abilene tackled him, shoving her head into his stomach, and upsetting the boy's aim.

42

So it was that Edward did not go flying back into the dirty hands of Martin.

Instead, Edward Tulane went overboard.

CHAPTER SIX

How does a china rabbit die?

Can a china rabbit drown?

Is my hat still on my head?

These were the questions that Edward asked himself as he went sailing out over the blue sea. The sun was high in the sky, and from what seemed to be a very long way away, Edward heard Abilene call his name.

"Edwaaarrd," she shouted, "come back."

Come back? Of all the ridiculous things to shout, thought Edward.

As he tumbled, ears over tail through the air, he managed to catch one last glimpse of Abilene.

He sank and sank and sank.

She was standing on the deck of the ship, holding on to the railing with one hand. In her other hand was a lamp—no, it was a ball of fire—no, Edward realized, it was his gold pocket watch that Abilene held in her hand; she was holding it up high, and it was reflecting the light of the sun.

My pocket watch, he thought. I need that.

And then Abilene disappeared from view and the rabbit hit the water with such tremendous force that his hat blew off his head.

That answers that question, thought Edward as he watched the hat dance away on the wind.

And then he began to sink.

He sank and sank and sank. He kept his eyes open the whole time. Not because he was brave, but because he had no choice. His painted-on eyes witnessed the blue water turning to green and then to blue again. They watched as it finally became as black as night.

Edward went down and down. He said to

himself, If I am going to drown, certainly I would have done so by now.

Far above him, the ocean liner, with Abilene aboard it, sailed blithely on; and the china rabbit landed, finally, on the ocean floor, face-down; and there, with his head in the muck, he experienced his first genuine and true emotion.

Edward Tulane was afraid.

CHAPTER SEVEN

HE TOLD HIMSELF THAT CERTAINLY Abilene would come and find him. This, Edward thought, is much like waiting for Abilene to come home from school. I will pretend that I am in the dining room of the house on Egypt Street, waiting for the little hand to move to the three and the big hand to land on the twelve. If only I had my watch, then I would know for sure. But it doesn't matter; she will be here soon, very soon.

Hours passed. And then days. And weeks. And months.

Abilene did not come.

Edward, for lack of anything better to do, began to think. He thought about the stars. He remembered what they looked like from his bedroom window.

What made them shine so brightly, he wondered, and were they still shining somewhere even though he could not see them? Never in my life, he thought, have I been farther away from the stars than I am now.

He considered, too, the fate of the beautiful princess who had become a warthog. Why had she become a warthog? Because the ugly witch turned her into one—that was why.

And then the rabbit thought about Pellegrina. He felt, in some way that he could not explain to himself, that she was responsible for what had happened to him. It was almost as if it was she, and not the boys, who had thrown Edward overboard.

She was like the witch in the story. No, she

was the witch in the story. True, she did not turn him into a warthog, but just the same she was punishing him, although for what he could not say.

On the two hundred and ninety-seventh day of Edward's ordeal, a storm came. The storm was so powerful that it lifted Edward off the ocean floor and led him in a crazy, wild and spinning dance. The water pummeled him and lifted him up and shoved him back down.

Help! thought Edward.

The storm, in its ferocity, actually flung him all the way out of the sea; and the rabbit glimpsed, for a moment, the light of an angry and bruised sky; the wind rushed through his ears. It sounded to him like Pellegrina laughing. But before he had time to appreciate being above water, he was tossed back down into the depths. Up and down, back and forth he went until the storm wore itself out, and Edward saw that he was beginning, again, his slow descent to the ocean floor.

Oh, help me, he thought. I can't go back there.
Help me.

But still, down he went. Down, down, down.

And then, suddenly, the great, wide net of a
fisherman reached out and grabbed the rabbit.
The net lifted him higher and higher until there
was an almost unbearable explosion of light and
Edward was back in the world, lying on the deck
of a ship, surrounded by fish.

"Eh, what's this?" said a voice.

"Ain't no fish," said another voice. "That's for
sure."

The light was so brilliant that it was hard for
Edward to see. But finally, shapes appeared out of
the light, and then faces. And Edward realized that
he was looking up at two men, one young and
one old.

"Looks like some toy," said the grizzled old
man. He bent and picked Edward up and held him

by his front paws, considering him. "A rabbit, I reckon. It's got whiskers. And rabbit ears, or the shape of rabbit ears at least."

"Yeah, sure, a rabbit toy," said the younger man, and he turned away.

"I'll take it home to Nellie. Let her fix it up and set it to rights. Give it to some child."

The old man placed Edward carefully on a crate, positioning him so that he was sitting up and could look out at the sea. Edward appreciated the courtesy of this small gesture, but he was heartily sick of the ocean and would have been satisfied never to set eyes on it again.

"There you go," said the old man.

As they made their way back to shore, Edward felt the sun on his face and the wind blowing through the little bit of fur left on his ears, and something filled his chest, a wonderful feeling.

He was glad to be alive.

"Look at that rabbit," the old man said. "Looks like it's enjoying the ride, don't it?"

"A-yep," said the young man.

In fact, Edward Tulane was so happy to be back among the living that he did not even take umbrage at being referred to as "it."

CHAPTER EIGHT

On land, the old fisherman stopped to light a pipe, and then, with the pipe clenched between his teeth, he walked home, carrying Edward atop his left shoulder as if he were a conquering hero. The fisherman balanced him there, placing a callused hand at Edward's back. He talked to him in a soft, low voice as they walked.

"You'll like Nellie, you will," said the old man. "She's had her sadness, but she's an all-right girl."

Edward looked at the small town blanketed in dusk: a jumble of buildings huddled together, the ocean stretching out in front of it all; and he thought that he would like anything and anybody that was not at the bottom of the sea.

"Hello, Lawrence," called a woman from the front of a shop. "What have you got?"

"Fresh catch," said the fisherman, "fresh rabbit from the sea." He lifted his cap to the lady and kept walking.

"There you are, now," said the fisherman. He took the pipe out of his mouth and pointed with the stem of it at a star in the purpling sky. "There's your North Star right there. Don't never have to be lost when you know where that fellow is."

Edward considered the brightness of the small star.

Do they all have names? he wondered.

"Listen at me," said the fisherman, "talking to a toy. Oh, well. Here we are, then." And with Edward still on his shoulder, the fisherman walked up a stone-lined path and into a little green house.

"Look here, Nellie," he said. "I've brought you something from the sea."

"I don't want nothing from the sea," came a voice.

"Aw, now, don't be like that, Nell. Come and see, then."

An old woman stepped out of the kitchen, wiping her hands on an apron. When she saw Edward, she dropped the apron and clapped her hands together and said, "Oh, Lawrence, you brung me a rabbit."

"Direct from the sea," said Lawrence. He took Edward off his shoulder and stood him up on the floor and held on to his hands and made him take a deep bow in the direction of Nellie.

"Oh," said Nellie, "here." She clapped her hands together again and Lawrence passed Edward to her.

Nellie held the rabbit out in front of her and looked him over from tip to toe. She smiled.

"SHE'S BEAUTIFUL," BREATHED NELLIE.

"Have you ever in your life seen anything so fine?" she said.

Edward felt immediately that Nellie was a very discerning woman.

"She's beautiful," breathed Nellie.

For a moment, Edward was confused. Was there some other object of beauty in the room?

"What will I call her?"

"Susanna?" said Lawrence.

"Just right," said Nellie. "Susanna." She looked deep into Edward's eyes. "First off, Susanna will need some clothes, won't she?"

CHAPTER NINE

AND SO EDWARD TULANE BECAME
Susanna. Nellie sewed several outfits for him: a pink
dress with ruffles for special occasions, a simple
shift fashioned out of a flower-covered cloth for
everyday use, and a long white gown made of
cotton for Edward to sleep in. In addition, she
remade his ears, stripping them of the few pieces
of fur that remained and designing him a new pair.

"Oh," she told him when she was done, "you
look lovely."

He was horrified at first. He was, after all, a
boy rabbit. He did not want to be dressed as a girl.
And the outfits, even the special-occasion dress,

were so simple, so plain. They lacked the elegance and artistry of his real clothes. But then Edward remembered lying on the ocean floor, the muck in his face, the stars so far away, and he said to himself, What difference does it make really? Wearing a dress won't hurt me.

Besides, life in the little green house with the fisherman and his wife was sweet. Nellie loved to bake, and so she spent her day in the kitchen. She put Edward on the counter and leaned him up against the flour canister and arranged his dress around his knees. She bent his ears so that he could hear well.

And then she set to work, kneading dough for bread and rolling out dough for cookies and pies. The kitchen soon filled with the smell of baking bread and with the sweet smells of cinnamon and sugar and cloves. The windows steamed up. And while Nellie worked, she talked.

She told Edward about her children, her

daughter, Lolly, who was a secretary, and her boys: Ralph, who was in the army, and Raymond, who had died of pneumonia when he was only five years old.

"He drowned inside of himself," said Nellie. "It is a horrible, terrible thing, the worst thing, to watch somebody you love die right in front of you and not be able to do nothing about it. I dream about him most nights."

Nellie wiped at her tears with the back of her hands. She smiled at Edward.

"I suppose you think I'm daft, talking to a toy. But it seems to me that you are listening, Susanna."

And Edward was surprised to discover that he was listening. Before, when Abilene talked to him, everything had seemed so boring, so pointless. But now, the stories Nellie told struck him as the most important thing in the world and he listened as if his life depended on what she said. It made him wonder if some of the muck from the ocean floor had gotten inside his china head and damaged him somehow.

In the evening, Lawrence came home from the sea and there was dinner and Edward sat at the table with the fisherman and his wife. He sat in an old wooden highchair; and while at first he was mortified (a highchair, after all, was a chair designed for babies, not for elegant rabbits), he soon became used to it. He liked being up high, looking out over the table instead of staring at the tablecloth as he had at the Tulane household. He liked feeling like a part of things.

Every night after dinner, Lawrence said that he thought he would go out and get some fresh air and that maybe Susanna would like to come with him. He placed Edward on his shoulder as he had that first night when he walked him through town, bringing him home to Nellie.

They went outside and Lawrence lit his pipe and held Edward there on his shoulder; and if the night was clear, Lawrence said the names of the constellations one at a time, Andromeda, Pegasus, pointing at them with the stem of his pipe. Edward loved looking up at the stars, and he loved the sounds of the constellation names. They were sweet in his ears.

Sometimes, though, staring up at the night sky, Edward remembered Pellegrina, saw again her dark and glowing eyes, and a chill would go through him.

Warthogs, he would think. Witches.

But Nellie, before she put him to bed each night, sang Edward a lullaby, a song about a mockingbird that did not sing and a diamond ring that would not shine, and the sound of Nellie's voice soothed the rabbit and he forgot about Pellegrina.

Life, for a very long time, was sweet.

And then Lawrence and Nellie's daughter came for a visit.

CHAPTER TEN

LOLLY WAS A LUMPY WOMAN WHO
spoke too loudly and who wore too much lipstick.
She entered the house and immediately spotted
Edward sitting on the living-room couch.

"What's this?" she said. She put down her
suitcase and picked Edward up by one foot. She
held him upside down.

"That's Susanna," said Nellie.

"Susanna!" shouted Lolly. She gave Edward
a shake.

His dress was up over his head and he could
see nothing. Already, he had formed a deep and
abiding hatred for Lolly.

"Your father found her," said Nellie. "She came up in a net and she didn't have no clothes on her, so I made her some dresses."

"Have you gone skivvy?" shouted Lolly. "Rabbits don't need clothes."

"Well," said Nellie. Her voice shook. "This one seemed to."

Lolly tossed Edward back on the couch. He landed face-down with his arms over his head and his dress still over his face, and he stayed that way through dinner.

"Why have you got out that old highchair?" shouted Lolly.

"Oh, don't pay it no mind," said Nellie. "Your father was just gluing on a missing piece, wasn't you, Lawrence?"

"That's right," said Lawrence, without looking up from his plate.

Of course, after dinner Edward did not go outside and stand beneath the stars to have a smoke with Lawrence. And Nellie, for the first time since Edward had been with her, did not sing him a lullaby. In fact, Edward was ignored and forgotten about until the next morning, when Lolly picked him up again and pulled his dress down away from his face and stared him in the eye.

"Got the old folks bewitched, don't you?" said Lolly. "I heard the talk in town. That they've been treating you like a rabbit child."

Edward stared back at Lolly. Her lipstick was a bright and bloody red. He felt a cold breeze blow through the room.

Was a door open somewhere?

"Well, you don't fool me," she said. She gave him a shake. "We'll be taking a trip together, you and me."

Holding Edward by the ears, Lolly marched into the kitchen and shoved him face-down in the garbage can.

"Ma!" Lolly shouted, "I'm taking the truck. I'm going to head on out and do some errands."

"Oh," came Nellie's tremulous voice, "that's wonderful, dear. Goodbye, then."

Goodbye, thought Edward as Lolly hauled the garbage can out to the truck.

"Goodbye," Nellie called again, louder this time.

Edward felt a sharp pain somewhere deep inside his china chest.

For the first time, his heart called out to him.

It said two words: Nellie. Lawrence.

CHAPTER ELEVEN

Edward ended up at the dump.
He lay on top of orange peels, coffee grounds, rancid bacon, and rubber tires. The first night, he was at the top of the garbage heap, and so he was able to look up at the stars and find comfort in their light.

In the morning, a short man came climbing through the trash and rubble. He stopped when he was standing on top of the highest pile. He put his hands under his armpits and flapped his elbows.

The man crowed loudly. He shouted, "Who am I? I'm Ernest, Ernest who is king of the world. How can I be king of the world? Because I am king of garbages. And garbages is what the world is made of. Ha. Ha, ha! Therefore, I am Ernest, Ernest who is king of the world." He crowed again.

Edward was inclined to agree with Ernest's assessment of the world being made of garbage, especially after his second day at the dump, when a load of trash was deposited directly on top of him. He lay there, buried alive. He could not see the sky. He could not see the stars. He could see nothing.

What kept Edward going, what gave him hope, was thinking of how he would find Lolly and exact his revenge. He would pick *her* up by the ears! He would bury *her* under a mountain of trash!

But after almost forty days and nights had passed, the weight and the smell of the garbage above and below him clouded Edward's thoughts, and soon he gave up thinking about revenge and gave in to despair. It was worse, much worse, than being buried at sea. It was worse because Edward was a different rabbit now. He couldn't say how he was different; he just knew that he was. He remembered, again, Pellegrina's story about the princess who had loved nobody. The witch turned her into a warthog *because* she loved nobody. He understood that now.

He heard Pellegrina say: "You disappoint me."

Why? he asked her. Why do I disappoint you?

But he knew the answer to that question, too. It was because he had not loved Abilene enough. And now she was gone from him. And he would never be able to make it right. And Nellie and Lawrence were gone, too. He missed them terribly. He wanted to be with them.

The rabbit wondered if that was love.

Day after day passed, and Edward was aware of time passing only because every morning he could hear Ernest performing his dawn ritual, cackling and crowing about being king of the world.

On his one hundred and eightieth day at the dump, salvation arrived for Edward in a most unusual form. The garbage around him shifted, and the rabbit heard the sniffing and panting of a dog. Then came the frenzied sound of digging. The garbage shifted again, and suddenly, miraculously, the beautiful, buttery light of late afternoon shone on Edward's face.

CHAPTER TWELVE

Edward did not have much time to savor the light, for the dog suddenly appeared above him, dark and shaggy, blocking his view. Edward was pulled out of the garbage by his ears, dropped, and then picked up again, this time around the middle, and shaken back and forth with a great deal of ferocity.

The little dog growled deep in its throat and then dropped Edward again and looked him in the eye. Edward stared back.

"Hey, get out of here, you dog!" It was Ernest, king of garbages and therefore king of the world.

The dog grabbed Edward by his pink dress and took off running.

"That's mine, that's mine, all garbages is mine!" Ernest shouted. "You come back here!"

But the little dog did not stop.

The sun was shining and Edward felt exhilarated. Who, having known him before, would have thought that he could be so happy now, crusted over with garbage, wearing a dress, held in the slobbery mouth of a dog and being chased by a mad man?

But he was happy.

The dog ran and ran until they reached a railroad track. They crossed over the tracks, and there, underneath a scraggly tree, in a circle of bushes, Edward was dropped in front of a large pair of feet.

The dog began to bark.

Edward looked up and saw that the feet were attached to an enormous man with a long, dark beard.

"What's this, Lucy?" said the man.

He bent and picked up Edward. He held him firmly around the middle. "Lucy," said the man, "I know how much you enjoy rabbit pie."

Lucy barked.

"Yes, yes, I know. Rabbit pie is a true delight, one of the pleasures of our existence."

Lucy let out a hopeful yip.

"And what we have here, what you have so graciously delivered to me, is definitely a rabbit, but the best chef in the world would be hard-pressed to make him into a pie."

Lucy growled.

"This rabbit is made of china, girl." The man held Edward closer to him. They looked each other in the eye. "You're made of china, aren't you, Malone?" He gave Edward a playful shake. "You are some child's toy, am I right? And you have been separated, somehow, from the child who loves you."

Edward felt, again, the sharp pain in his chest. He thought of Abilene. He saw the path leading up to the house on Egypt Street. He saw the dusk descending and Abilene running toward him.

Yes, Abilene had loved him.

"So, Malone," said the man. He cleared his throat. "You are lost. That is my guess. Lucy and I are lost, too."

At the sound of her name, Lucy let out another yip.

"Perhaps," said the man, "you would like to be lost with us. I have found it much more agreeable to be lost in the company of others. My name is Bull. Lucy, as you may have surmised, is my dog. Would you care to join us?"

Bull waited for a moment, staring at Edward; and then with his hands still firmly around Edward's waist, the man reached one enormous finger up and touched Edward's head from behind. He pushed it so it looked as if Edward were nodding his head in agreement.

"Look, Lucy. He is saying yes," said Bull. "Malone has agreed to travel with us. Isn't that swell?"

Lucy danced around Bull's feet, wagging her tail and barking.

And so it was that Edward took to the road with a hobo and his dog.

Chapter Thirteen

THEY TRAVELED ON FOOT. THEY traveled in empty railcars. They were always on the move.

"But in truth," said Bull, "we are going nowhere. That, my friend, is the irony of our constant movement."

Edward rode in Bull's bedroll, slung over Bull's shoulder with only his head and ears sticking out. Bull was always careful to position the rabbit so that he was not looking down or up, but was, instead, forever looking behind him, at the road they had just traveled.

At night, they slept on the ground, under the stars. Lucy, after her initial disappointment about Edward being unfit for consumption, took a liking to him and slept curled up beside him; sometimes, she even rested her muzzle on his china stomach, and then the noises she made in her sleep, whimpering and growling and chuffing, resonated inside Edward's body. To his surprise, he began to feel a deep tenderness for the dog.

During the night, while Bull and Lucy slept, Edward, with his ever-open eyes, stared up at the constellations. He said their names, and then he said the names of the people who loved him. He started with Abilene and then went to Nellie and Lawrence and from there to Bull and Lucy, and then he ended again with Abilene: Abilene, Nellie, Lawrence, Bull, Lucy, Abilene.

See? Edward told Pellegrina. I am not like the princess. I know about love.

There were times, too, when Bull and Lucy

EDWARD LOVED IT WHEN BULL SANG.

gathered around a campfire with other tramps. Bull was a good storyteller and an even better singer.

"Sing for us, Bull," the men shouted.

Bull sat with Lucy leaning against his leg and Edward balanced on his right knee and he sang from somewhere deep inside himself. Just as Edward could feel Lucy's whimpers and growls resonate through his body at night, he could also feel the deep, sad sound of Bull's songs move through him. Edward loved it when Bull sang.

And he was grateful to Bull, too, for sensing that a dress was not the right kind of clothing for Edward.

"Malone," said Bull one night, "it's not my desire to offend you or to comment negatively on your choice of garb, but I'm forced to tell you that you stick out like a sore thumb in that princess dress. And also, again, with no wish to offend you, the dress has seen better days."

Nellie's beautiful dress had not fared well at the dump or in its subsequent ramblings with Bull and Lucy. It was so torn and dirty and full of holes that it barely resembled a dress anymore.

"I have a solution," said Bull, "and I hope that it meets with your approval."

He took his own knit stocking cap and cut a big hole in the top of it and two small holes on the side of it and then he took off Edward's dress.

"Look away, Lucy," he said to the dog, "let's not embarrass Malone by staring at his naked-ness." Bull slid the hat over Edward's head and pulled it down and poked his arms through the smaller holes. "There you go," he said to Edward. "Now you just need some pants."

The pants Bull made himself, cutting up several red handkerchiefs and sewing them together so that they formed a makeshift covering for Edward's long legs.

"Now you have the proper outlaw look," said Bull, standing back to admire his work. "Now you look like a rabbit on the run."

CHAPTER FOURTEEN

AT FIRST, THE OTHERS THOUGHT that Edward was a great good joke.

"A rabbit," the hoboes said, laughing. "Let's chop him up and put him in the stew pot."

Or when Bull sat with Edward carefully balanced on his knee, one of them would call out, "Got yourself a little dolly, Bull?"

Edward, of course, felt a surge of anger at being referred to as a dolly. But Bull never got angry. He simply sat with Edward on his knee and said nothing. Soon, the men became accustomed to Edward, and word of his existence spread. So it was that when Bull and Lucy stepped up to a campfire in another town, another state, another place entirely, the men knew Edward and were glad to see him.

"Malone!" they shouted in unison.

And Edward felt a warm rush of pleasure at being recognized, at being known.

Whatever it was that had begun in Nellie's kitchen, Edward's new and strange ability to sit very still and concentrate the whole of his being on the stories of another, became invaluable around the hobo campfire.

"Look at Malone," said a man named Jack one evening. "He's listening to every dang word."

"Certainly," said Bull, "of course he is."

Later that night, Jack came and sat next to Bull and asked if he could borrow the rabbit. Bull handed Edward over, and Jack sat with Edward upon his knee. He whispered in Edward's ear.

"Helen," Jack said, "and Jack Junior and Taffy—she's the baby. Those are my kids' names. They are all in North Carolina. You ever been to North Carolina? It's a pretty state. That's where they are. Helen. Jack Junior. Taffy. You remember their names, okay, Malone?"

After this, wherever Bull and Lucy and Edward went, some tramp would take Edward aside and whisper the names of his children in Edward's ear. Betty. Ted. Nancy. William. Jimmy. Eileen. Skipper. Faith.

Edward knew what it was like to say over and over again the names of those you had left behind. He knew what it was like to miss someone. And so he listened. And in his listening, his heart opened wide and then wider still.

The rabbit stayed lost with Lucy and Bull for a long time. Almost seven years passed, and in that time, Edward became an excellent tramp: happy to be on the road, restless when he was still. The sound of the wheels on the train tracks became a music that soothed him. He could have ridden the rails forever. But one night, in a railroad yard in Memphis, as Bull and Lucy slept in an empty freight car and Edward kept watch, trouble arrived.

A man entered the freight car and shone a flashlight in Bull's face and then kicked him awake.

"You bum," he said, "you dirty bum. I'm sick of you guys sleeping everywhere. This ain't no motel."

Bull sat up slowly. Lucy started to bark.

"Shut up," said the man. He delivered a swift kick to Lucy's side that made her yelp in surprise.

All his life, Edward had known what he was: a rabbit made of china, a rabbit with bendable arms and legs and ears. He was bendable, though, only if he was in the hands of another. He could not move himself. And he had never regretted this more deeply than he did that night when he and Bull and Lucy were discovered in the empty railcar. Edward wanted to be able to defend Lucy. But he could do nothing. He could only lie there and wait.

"Say something," said the man to Bull.

Bull put his hands up in the air. He said, "We are lost."

"Lost, ha. You bet you're lost." And then the man said, "What's this?" and he shone the light on Edward.

"That's Malone," said Bull.

"What the heck?" said the man. He poked at Edward with the toe of his boot. "Things are out of control. Things are out of hand. Not on my watch. No, sir. Not when I'm in charge."

The train suddenly lurched into motion.

"No, sir," said the man again. He looked down at Edward. "No free rides for rabbits." He turned and flung open the door of the railcar, and then he turned back and with one swift kick, he sent Edward sailing out into the darkness.

The rabbit flew through the late spring air.

From far behind him, he heard Lucy's anguished howl.

Arrooooooooooo, ahhhhrrrrrrooo, she cried.

Edward landed with a most alarming *thump,* and then he tumbled and tumbled and tumbled down a long dirty hill. When he finally stopped moving, he was on his back, staring up at the night sky. The world was silent. He could not hear Lucy. He could not hear the train.

Edward looked up at the stars. He started to say the names of the constellations, but then he stopped.

"Bull," his heart said. "Lucy."

How many times, Edward wondered, would he have to leave without getting the chance to say goodbye?

A lone cricket started up a song.

Edward listened.

Something deep inside him ached.

He wished that he could cry.

CHAPTER FIFTEEN

In the morning, the sun rose and the cricket song gave way to bird song and an old woman came walking down the dirt road and tripped right over Edward.

"Hmph," she said. She pushed at Edward with her fishing pole.

"Looks like a rabbit," she said. She put down her basket and bent and stared at Edward. "Only he ain't real."

She stood back up. "Hmph," she said again. She rubbed her back. "What I say is, there's a use for everything and everything has its use. That's what I say."

Edward didn't care what she said. The terrible ache he had felt the night before had gone away and had been replaced with a different feeling, one of hollowness and despair.

Pick me up or don't pick me up, the rabbit thought. It makes no difference to me.

The old lady picked him up.

She bent him double and put him in her basket, which smelled of weeds and fish, and then she kept walking, swinging the basket and singing, "Nobody knows the troubles I seen."

Edward, in spite of himself, listened.

I've seen troubles, too, he thought. You bet I have. And apparently they aren't over yet.

Edward was right. His troubles were not over.

The old woman found a use for him.

She hung him from a pole in her vegetable garden. She nailed his velvet ears to the wooden pole and spread his arms out as if he were flying and attached his paws to the pole by wrapping pieces of wire around them. In addition to Edward, pie tins hung from the pole. They clinked and clanked and shone in the morning sun.

"Ain't a doubt in my mind that you can scare them off," the old lady said.

Scare who off? Edward wondered.

Birds, he soon discovered.

Crows. They came flying at him, cawing and screeching, wheeling over his head, diving at his ears.

"Go on, Clyde," said the woman. She clapped her hands. "You got to act ferocious."

Clyde? Edward felt a weariness so intense wash over him that he thought he might actually be able to sigh aloud. Would the world never tire of calling him by the wrong name?

The old woman clapped her hands again. "Get to work, Clyde," she said. "Scare them birds off." And then she walked away from him, out of the garden and toward her small house.

I HAVE BEEN LOVED, EDWARD TOLD THE STARS.

The birds were insistent. They flew around his head. They tugged at the loose threads in his sweater. One large crow in particular would not leave the rabbit alone. He perched on the pole and screamed a dark message in Edward's left ear: *Caw, caw, caw,* without ceasing. As the sun rose higher and shone meaner and brighter, Edward became somewhat dazed. He mistook the large crow for Pellegrina.

Go ahead, he thought. Turn me into a warthog if you want. I don't care. I am done with caring.

Caw, caw, said the Pellegrina crow.

Finally, the sun set and the birds flew away. Edward hung by his velvet ears and looked up at the night sky. He saw the stars. But for the first time in his life, he looked at them and felt no comfort. Instead, he felt mocked. You are down there alone, the stars seemed to say to him. And we are up here, in our constellations, together.

I have been loved, Edward told the stars.

So? said the stars. What difference does that make when you are all alone now?

Edward could think of no answer to that question.

Eventually, the sky lightened and the stars disappeared one by one. The birds returned and the old woman came back to the garden.

She brought a boy with her.

CHAPTER SIXTEEN

B RYCE," SAID THE OLD WOMAN, "GIT away from that rabbit. I ain't paying you to stand and stare."

"Yes, ma'am," said Bryce. He wiped his nose with the back of his hand and continued to look up at Edward. The boy's eyes were brown with flecks of gold shining in them.

"Hey," he whispered to Edward.

A crow settled on Edward's head, and the boy flapped his arms and shouted, "Go on, git!" and the bird spread his wings and flew away.

"Bryce!" shouted the old woman.

"Ma'am?" said Bryce.

"Git away from that rabbit. Do your work. I ain't gonna say it again."

"Yes'm," said Bryce. He wiped his hand across his nose. "I'll be back to get you," he said to Edward.

The rabbit spent the day hanging by his ears, baking in the hot sun, watching the old woman and Bryce weed and hoe the garden. Whenever the woman wasn't looking, Bryce raised his hand and waved.

The birds circled over Edward's head, laughing at him.

What was it like to have wings? Edward wondered. If he had had wings when he was tossed overboard, he would not have sunk to the bottom of the sea. Instead, he would have flown in the opposite direction, up, into the deep, bright blue sky. And when Lolly took him to the dump, he would have flown out of the garbage and followed her and landed on her head, holding on with his sharp claws. And on the train, when the man kicked him, Edward would not have fallen to the ground; instead he would have risen up and sat on top of the train and laughed at the man: *Caw, caw, caw.*

In the late afternoon, Bryce and the old lady left the field. Bryce winked at Edward as he walked past him. One of the crows lighted on Edward's shoulder and tapped with his beak at Edward's china face, reminding the rabbit with each tap that he had no wings, that not only could he not fly, he could not move on his own at all, in any way.

Dusk descended over the field, and then came true dark. A whippoorwill sang out over and over again. *Whip poor Will. Whip poor Will.* It was the saddest sound Edward had ever heard. And then came another song, the hum of a harmonica.

Bryce stepped out of the shadows.

"Hey," he said to Edward. He wiped his nose

with the back of his hand and then played another bit of song on the harmonica. "I bet you didn't think I'd come back. But here I am. I come to save you."

Too late, thought Edward as Bryce climbed the pole and worked at the wires that were tied around his wrists. I am nothing but a hollow rabbit.

Too late, thought Edward as Bryce pulled the nails out of his ears. I am only a doll made of china.

But when the last nail was out and he fell forward into Bryce's arms, the rabbit felt a rush of relief, and the feeling of relief was followed by one of joy.

Perhaps, he thought, it is not too late, after all, for me to be saved.

CHAPTER SEVENTEEN

Bryce slung Edward over his shoulder. He started to walk.

"I come to get you for Sarah Ruth," Bryce said. "You don't know Sarah Ruth. She's my sister. She's sick. She had her a baby doll made out of china. She loved that baby doll. But he broke it.

"He *broke* it. He was drunk and stepped on that baby's head and smashed it into a hundred million pieces. Them pieces was so small, I couldn't make them go back together. I couldn't. I tried and tried."

At this point in his story, Bryce stopped walking and shook his head and wiped at his nose with the back of his hand.

"Sarah Ruth ain't had nothing to play with since. He won't buy her nothing. He says she don't need nothing. He says she don't need nothing because she ain't gonna live. But he don't know."

Bryce started to walk again. "He don't know," he said.

Who "he" was, was not clear to Edward. What was clear was that he was being taken to a child to make up for the loss of a doll. A doll. How Edward loathed dolls. And to be thought of as a likely replacement for a doll offended him. But still, it was, he had to admit, a highly preferable alternative to hanging by his ears from a post.

The house in which Bryce and Sarah Ruth lived was so small and crooked that Edward did not believe, at first, that it was a house. He mistook it, instead, for a chicken coop. Inside, there were two beds and a kerosene lamp and not much else. Bryce laid Edward at the foot of one of the beds and then lit the lamp.

"Sarah," Bryce whispered, "Sarah Ruth. You got to wake up now, honey. I brung you something." He took the harmonica out of his pocket and played the beginning of a simple melody.

The little girl sat up in her bed and immediately started to cough. Bryce put his hand on her back. "That's all right," he told her. "That's okay."

She was young, maybe four years old, and she had white-blond hair, and even in the poor light of the lamp, Edward could see that her eyes were the same gold-flecked brown as Bryce's.

"That's right," said Bryce. "You go on ahead and cough."

Sarah Ruth obliged him. She coughed and coughed and coughed. On the wall of the cabin, the kerosene light cast her trembling shadow, hunched over and small. The coughing was the saddest sound that Edward had ever heard, sadder even than the mournful call of the whippoorwill. Finally, Sarah Ruth stopped.

Bryce said, "You want to see what I brung you?"

Sarah Ruth nodded.

"You got to close your eyes."

The girl closed her eyes.

Bryce picked up Edward and held him so that he was standing straight, like a soldier, at the end of the bed. "All right now, you can open them."

Sarah Ruth opened her eyes, and Bryce moved Edward's china legs and china arms so it looked as if he were dancing.

Sarah Ruth laughed and clapped her hands. "Rabbit," she said.

"He's for you, honey," said Bryce.

Sarah Ruth looked first at Edward and then at

Bryce and then back at Edward again, her eyes wide and disbelieving.

"He's yours."

"Mine?"

Sarah Ruth, Edward was soon to discover, rarely said more than one word at a time. Words, at least several of them strung together, made her cough. She limited herself. She said only what needed to be said.

"Yours," said Bryce. "I got him special for you."

This knowledge provoked another fit of coughing in Sarah Ruth, and she hunched over again. When the fit was done, she uncurled herself and held out her arms.

"That's right," said Bryce. He handed Edward to her.

"Baby," said Sarah Ruth.

She rocked Edward back and forth and stared down at him and smiled.

Never in his life had Edward been cradled like

"HUSH," SHE SAID TO EDWARD AS SHE ROCKED HIM BACK AND FORTH.

a baby. Abilene had not done it. Nor had Nellie. And most certainly Bull had not. It was a singular sensation to be held so gently and yet so fiercely, to be stared down at with so much love. Edward felt the whole of his china body flood with warmth.

"You going to give him a name, honey?" Bryce asked.

"Jangles," said Sarah Ruth without taking her eyes off Edward.

"Jangles, huh? That's a good name. I like that name."

Bryce patted Sarah Ruth on the head. She continued to stare down at Edward.

"Hush," she said to Edward as she rocked him back and forth.

"From the minute I first seen him," said Bryce, "I knew he belonged to you. I said to myself, 'That rabbit is for Sarah Ruth, for sure.'"

"Jangles," murmured Sarah Ruth.

Outside the cabin, thunder cracked and then

came the sound of rain falling on the tin roof. Sarah Ruth rocked Edward back and forth, back and forth, and Bryce took out his harmonica and started to play, making his song keep rhythm with the rain.

Chapter Eighteen

BRYCE AND SARAH RUTH HAD A
father.

Early the next morning, when the light was gray and uncertain, Sarah Ruth was sitting up in bed, coughing, and the father came home. He picked Edward up by one of his ears and said, "I ain't never."

"It's a baby doll," said Bryce.

"Don't look like no baby doll to me."

Edward, hanging by one ear, was frightened. This, he was certain, was the man who crushed the heads of china dolls.

"Jangles," said Sarah Ruth between coughs. She held out her arms.

"He's hers," said Bryce. "He belongs to her."

The father dropped Edward on the bed, and Bryce picked up the rabbit and handed him to Sarah Ruth.

"It don't matter anyway," said the father. "It don't make no difference. None of it."

"It does so matter," said Bryce.

"Don't you sass me," said the father. He raised his hand and slapped Bryce across his mouth and then he turned and left the house.

"You ain't got to worry about him," said Bryce to Edward. "He ain't nothing but a bully. And besides, he don't hardly ever come home."

Fortunately, the father did not come back that day. Bryce went out to work and Sarah Ruth spent the day in bed, holding Edward in her lap and playing with a box filled with buttons.

"Pretty," she said to Edward as she lined up

the buttons on the bed and arranged them into different patterns.

Sometimes, when a coughing fit was particularly bad, she squeezed Edward so tight that he was afraid he would crack in two. Also, in between coughing fits, she took to sucking on one or the other of Edward's ears. Normally, Edward would have found intrusive, clingy behavior of this sort very annoying, but there was something about Sarah Ruth. He wanted to take care of her. He wanted to protect her. He wanted to do *more* for her.

At the end of the day, Bryce returned with a biscuit for Sarah Ruth and a ball of twine for Edward.

Sarah Ruth held the biscuit in both hands and took small, tentative bites.

"You eat that all up, honey. Let me hold Jangles," said Bryce. "Him and me got a surprise for you."

Bryce took Edward off in a corner of the room, and with his pocketknife, he cut off lengths of twine and tied them to Edward's arms and feet and then tied the twine to sticks of wood.

"See, all day I been thinking about it," Bryce said, "what we're going to do is make you dance. Sarah Ruth loves dancing. Mama used to hold on to her and dance her around the room.

"You eating that biscuit?" Bryce called out to Sarah Ruth.

"Uh-huh," said Sarah Ruth.

"You hold on, honey. We got a surprise for you." Bryce stood up. "Close your eyes," he told her. He took Edward over to the bed and said, "Okay, you can open them now."

Sarah Ruth opened her eyes.

"Dance, Jangles," said Bryce. And then, moving the strings with the sticks with his one hand, Bryce made Edward dance and drop and sway. And the whole while, at the same time, with his other hand, he held on to the harmonica and played a bright and lively tune.

Sarah Ruth laughed. She laughed until she started to cough, and then Bryce laid Edward down and took Sarah Ruth in his lap and rocked her and rubbed her back.

"You want some fresh air?" he asked her. "Let's get you out of this nasty old air, huh?"

Bryce carried his sister outside. He left Edward lying on the bed, and the rabbit, staring up at the smoke-stained ceiling, thought again about having wings. If he had them, he thought, he would fly high above the world, to where the air was clear and sweet, and he would take Sarah Ruth with him. He would carry her in his arms. Surely, so high above the world, she would be able to breathe without coughing.

After a minute, Bryce came back inside, still carrying Sarah Ruth.

"She wants you, too," he said.

"Jangles," said Sarah Ruth. She held out her arms.

So Bryce held Sarah Ruth and Sarah Ruth held Edward and the three of them stood outside.

Bryce said, "You got to look for falling stars. Them are the ones with magic."

They were quiet for a long time, all three of them looking up at the sky. Sarah Ruth stopped coughing. Edward thought that maybe she had fallen asleep.

"There," she said. And she pointed to a star streaking through the night sky.

"Make a wish, honey," Bryce said, his voice high and tight. "That's your star. You make you a wish for anything you want."

And even though it was Sarah Ruth's star, Edward wished on it, too.

CHAPTER NINETEEN

THE DAYS PASSED. THE SUN ROSE and set and rose and set again and again. Sometimes the father came home and sometimes he did not. Edward's ears became soggy and he did not care. His sweater had almost completely unraveled and it didn't bother him. He was hugged half to death and it felt good. In the evenings, at the hands of Bryce, at the ends of the twine, Edward danced and danced.

One month passed and then two and then three. Sarah Ruth got worse. In the fifth month, she refused to eat. And in the sixth month, she began to cough up blood. Her breathing became ragged and uncertain, as if she was trying to remember, in between breaths, what to do, what breathing was.

"Breathe, honey," Bryce stood over her and said.

Breathe, thought Edward from deep inside the well of her arms. Please, please breathe.

Bryce stopped leaving the house. He sat at home all day and held Sarah Ruth in his lap and rocked her back and forth and sang to her; on a bright morning in September, Sarah Ruth stopped breathing.

"Oh no," said Bryce. "Oh, honey, take a little breath. Please."

Edward had fallen out of Sarah Ruth's arms the night before and she had not asked for him again. So, face-down on the floor, arms over his head, Edward listened as Bryce wept. He listened as the father came home and shouted at Bryce. He listened as the father wept.

"Come on, Jangles."

"You can't cry!" Bryce shouted. "You got no right to cry. You never even loved her. You don't know nothing about love."

"I loved her," said the father. "I loved her."

I loved her, too, thought Edward. I loved her and now she is gone. How could this be? he wondered. How could he bear to live in a world without Sarah Ruth?

The yelling between the father and son continued, and then there was a terrible moment when the father insisted that Sarah Ruth belonged to him, that she was his girl, his baby, and that he was taking her to be buried.

"She ain't yours!" Bryce screamed. "You can't take her. She ain't yours."

But the father was bigger and stronger, and he prevailed. He wrapped Sarah Ruth in a blanket and carried her away. The small house became very quiet. Edward could hear Bryce moving around, muttering to himself. And then, finally, the boy picked Edward up.

"Come on, Jangles," Bryce said. "We're leaving. We're going to Memphis."

CHAPTER TWENTY

HOW MANY DANCING RABBITS HAVE
you seen in your life?" Bryce said to Edward. "I
can tell you how many I seen. One. You. That's
how you and me are going to make some money.
I seen it the last time I was in Memphis. Folks
put on any kind of show right there on the street
corner and people pay 'em for it. I seen it."

The walk to town took all night. Bryce walked
without stopping, carrying Edward under one arm
and talking to him the whole time. Edward tried
to listen, but the terrible scarecrow feeling had
come back, the feeling he had when he was hanging by his ears in the old lady's garden, the feeling

that nothing mattered, and that nothing would ever matter again.

And not only did Edward feel hollow; he ached. Every part of his china body hurt. He ached for Sarah Ruth. He wanted her to hold him. He wanted to dance for her.

And he did dance, but it was not for Sarah Ruth. Edward danced for strangers on a dirty street corner in Memphis. Bryce played his harmonica and moved Edward's strings, and Edward bowed and shuffled and swayed and people stopped to stare and point and laugh. On the ground in front of them was Sarah Ruth's button box. The lid was open to encourage people to drop change inside it.

"Mama," said a small child, "look at that bunny. I want to touch him." He reached out his hand for Edward.

"No," said the mother, "dirty." She pulled the child back, away from Edward. "Nasty," she said.

A man wearing a hat stopped and stared at Edward and Bryce.

"It's a sin to dance," he said. And then after a long pause, he said, "It's a particular sin for rabbits to dance."

The man took off his hat and held it over his heart. He stood and watched the boy and the rabbit for a long time. Finally, he put his hat back on his head and walked away.

The shadows lengthened. The sun became an orange dusty ball low in the sky. Bryce started to cry. Edward saw his tears land on the pavement. But the boy did not stop playing his harmonica. He did not make Edward stop dancing.

An old woman leaning on a cane stepped up close to them. She stared at Edward with deep, dark eyes.

Pellegrina? thought the dancing rabbit.

She nodded at him.

Look at me, he said to her. His arms and legs

jerked. Look at me. You got your wish. I have learned how to love. And it's a terrible thing. I'm broken. My heart is broken. Help me.

The old woman turned and hobbled away.

Come back, thought Edward. Fix me.

Bryce cried harder. He made Edward dance faster.

Finally, when the sun was gone and the streets were dark, Bryce stopped playing his harmonica.

"I'm done now," he said.

He let Edward fall to the pavement. "I ain't gonna cry anymore." Bryce wiped his nose and his eyes with the back of his hand; he picked up the button box and looked inside it. "We got us enough money to get something to eat," he said. "Come on, Jangles."

CHAPTER TWENTY-ONE

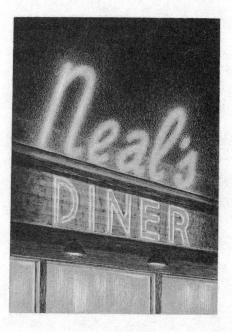

THE DINER WAS CALLED NEAL'S. THE
word was written in big, red neon letters that
flashed on and off. Inside, it was warm and bright
and smelled like fried chicken and toast and coffee.

Bryce sat at the counter and put Edward on a
stool next to him. He leaned the rabbit's forehead
up against the counter so that he would not fall.

"What you gonna have, sugar?" the waitress
said to Bryce.

"Give me some pancakes," said Bryce, "and
some eggs and I want steak, too. I want a big old
steak. And some toast. And some coffee."

The waitress leaned forward and pulled at one

of Edward's ears and then pushed him backward so that she could see his face.

"This your rabbit?" she said to Bryce.

"Yes'm. He's mine now. He belonged to my sister." Bryce wiped at his nose with the back of his hand. "We're in show business, me and him."

"Is that right?" said the waitress. She had a nametag on the front of her dress. *Marlene*, it said. She looked at Edward's face, and then she let go of his ear and he fell forward so that his head rested against the counter again.

Go ahead, Marlene, thought Edward. Push me around. Do with me as you will. What does it matter? I am broken. Broken.

The food came, and Bryce ate all of it without even looking up from his plate.

"Well, you was hungry for sure," said Marlene as she cleared away the plates. "I reckon show business is hard work."

"Yes'm," said Bryce.

Marlene tucked the check under the coffee cup. Bryce picked it up and looked at it and then shook his head.

"I ain't got enough," he said to Edward.

"Ma'am," he said to Marlene when she came back and filled up his coffee cup. "I ain't got enough."

"What, sugar?"

"I ain't got enough money."

She stopped pouring the coffee and looked at him. "You're going to have to talk to Neal about that."

Neal, it turned out, was both the owner and the cook. He was a large, red-haired, red-faced man who came out of the kitchen holding a spatula in one hand.

"You came in here hungry, right?" he said to Bryce.

"Yes, sir," said Bryce. He wiped his nose with the back of his hand.

"And you ordered some food and I cooked it and Marlene brought it to you. Right?"

"I reckon," said Bryce.

"You reckon?" said Neal. He brought the spatula down on the countertop with a *thwack.*

Bryce jumped. "Yes, sir. I mean, no sir."

"I. Cooked. It. For. You," said Neal.

"Yes, sir," said Bryce. He picked Edward up off the stool and held him close. Everyone in the diner had stopped eating. They were all staring at the boy and the rabbit and Neal. Only Marlene looked away.

"You ordered it. I cooked it. Marlene served it. You ate it. Now," said Neal. "I want my money." He tapped the spatula lightly on the counter.

Bryce cleared his throat. "You ever seen a rabbit dance?" he said.

"How's that?" said Neal.

"You ever before in your life seen a rabbit dance?" Bryce set Edward on the floor and started pulling the strings attached to his feet, making him do a slow shuffle. He put his harmonica in his mouth and played a sad song that went along with the dance.

Somebody laughed.

Bryce took the harmonica out of his mouth and said, "He could dance some more if you want him to. He could dance to pay for what I ate."

Neal stared at Bryce. And then without warning, he reached down and grabbed hold of Edward.

"This is what I think of dancing rabbits," said Neal.

And he swung Edward by the feet, swung him so that his head hit the edge of the counter hard.

There was a loud crack.

Bryce screamed.

And the world, Edward's world, went black.

CHAPTER TWENTY-TWO

IT WAS DUSK, AND EDWARD WAS walking down a sidewalk. He was walking on his own, putting one foot in front of the other without any assistance from anybody. He was wearing a fine suit made of red silk.

He walked down the sidewalk, and then he turned onto a path that led up to a house with lighted windows.

I know this house, thought Edward. This is Abilene's house. I am on Egypt Street.

Lucy came running out the front door of the house, barking and jumping and wagging her tail.

"Down, girl," said a deep, gruff voice.

Edward looked up and there was Bull, standing at the door.

"Hello, Malone," said Bull. "Hello, good old rabbit pie. We've been waiting for you." Bull swung the door wide and Edward walked inside.

Abilene was there, and Nellie and Lawrence and Bryce.

"Susanna," called Nellie.

"Jangles," said Bryce.

"Edward," said Abilene. She held out her arms to him.

But Edward stood still. He looked around the room.

"You searching for Sarah Ruth?" Bryce asked.

Edward nodded.

"You got to go outside if you want to see Sarah Ruth," said Bryce.

So they all went outside, Lucy and Bull and Nellie and Lawrence and Bryce and Abilene and Edward.

"Right there," said Bryce. He pointed up at the stars.

"Yep," said Lawrence, "that is the Sarah Ruth constellation." He picked Edward up and put him on his shoulder. "You can see it right there."

Edward felt a pang of sorrow, deep and sweet and familiar. Why did she have to be so far away?

If only I had wings, he thought, I could fly to her.

Out of the corner of his eye, the rabbit saw something flutter. Edward looked over his shoulder and there they were, the most magnificent wings he had ever seen, orange and red and blue and yellow. And they were on his back. They belonged to him. They were his wings.

What a wonderful night this was! He was walking on his own. He had an elegant new suit. And now he had wings. He could fly anywhere, do anything. Why had he never realized it before?

His heart soared inside of him. He spread his wings and flew off Lawrence's shoulders, out of his hands and up into the nighttime sky, toward the stars, toward Sarah Ruth.

"No!" shouted Abilene.

"Catch him," said Bryce.

Edward flew higher.

Lucy barked.

"Malone!" shouted Bull. And with a terrific lunge, he grabbed hold of Edward's feet and pulled him out of the sky and wrestled him to the earth. "You can't go yet," said Bull.

"Stay with us," said Abilene.

Edward beat his wings, but it was no use. Bull held him firmly to the ground.

"Stay with us," repeated Abilene.

Edward started to cry.

"I couldn't stand to lose you again," said Nellie.

"Neither could I," said Abilene. "It would break my heart."

Lucy bent her face to Edward's.

She licked his tears away.

CHAPTER TWENTY-THREE

EXCEEDINGLY WELL MADE," SAID
the man who was running a warm cloth over
Edward's face, "a work of art, I would say—
a surpassingly, unbelievably dirty work of art, but
art nonetheless. And dirt can be dealt with. Just as
your broken head has been dealt with."

Edward looked into the eyes of the man.

"Ah, there you are," the man said. "I can see
that you are listening now. Your head was broken.
I fixed it. I brought you back from the world of
the dead."

My heart, thought Edward, my *heart* is broken.

"No, no. No need to thank me," the man said. "It's my job, quite literally. Allow me to introduce myself. I am Lucius Clarke, doll mender. Your head . . . may I tell you? Will it upset you? Well, I always say the truth must be met head-on, no pun intended. Your head, young sir, was in twenty-one pieces."

Twenty-one pieces? Edward repeated mindlessly.

Lucius Clarke nodded. "Twenty-one," he said. "All modesty aside, I must admit that a lesser doll mender, a doll mender without my skills, might not have been able to rescue you. But let's not speak of what might have been. Let us speak instead of what is. You are whole. You have been pulled back from the brink of oblivion by your humble servant, Lucius Clarke." And here, Lucius Clarke put his hand on his chest and bowed deeply over Edward.

This was quite a speech to wake up to, and Edward lay on his back trying to absorb it. He was on a wooden table. He was in a room with sunshine pouring in from high windows. His head, apparently, had been in twenty-one pieces and now was put back together into one. He was not wearing a red suit. In fact, he had no clothes on at all. He was naked again. And he did not have wings.

And then he remembered: Bryce, the diner, Neal swinging him through the air.

Bryce.

"You are wondering, perhaps, about your young friend," said Lucius, "the one with the continually running nose. Yes. He brought you here, weeping, begging for my assistance. 'Put him together again,' he said. 'Put him back together.'

"I told him, I said, 'Young sir, I am a businessman. I can put your rabbit back together again.

For a price. The question is, can you pay this price?' He could not. Of course, he could not. He said that he could not.

"I told him then that he had two options. Only two. The first option being that he seek assistance elsewhere. Option two was that I would fix you to the very best of my considerable abilities and then you would become mine—his no longer, but mine."

Here Lucius fell silent. He nodded, agreeing with himself. "Two options only," he said. "And your friend chose option two. He gave you up so that you could be healed. Extraordinary, really."

Bryce, thought Edward.

Lucius Clarke clapped his hands together. "But no worries, my friend. No worries. I fully intend to keep up my end of the bargain. I will restore you to what I perceive to be your former glory. You shall have rabbit-fur ears and a rabbit-fur tail. Your whiskers will be repaired and replaced, your eyes repainted to a bright and stunning blue. You will be clothed in the finest of suits.

"And then, someday, I will reap the return on my investment in you. All in good time. All in good time. In the doll business, we have a saying: there is real time and there is doll time. You, my fine friend, have entered doll time."

CHAPTER TWENTY-FOUR

AND SO EDWARD TULANE WAS
mended, put together again, cleaned and polished,
dressed in an elegant suit and placed on a high
shelf for display. From this shelf, Edward could
see the whole shop: Lucius Clarke's workbench
and the windows to the outside world and the
door that the customers used to enter and leave.
From this shelf, Edward saw Bryce open the door
one day and stand in the threshold, the silver
harmonica in his left hand flashing brilliantly in
the sunlight flooding in through the windows.

"Young sir," said Lucius, "I am afraid that we
made a deal."

"You may look and then you must go and not come back."

"Can't I see him?" asked Bryce. He wiped his hand across his nose and the gesture filled Edward with a terrible feeling of love and loss. "I just want to look at him."

Lucius Clarke sighed. "You may look," he said. "You may look and then you must go and not come back. I cannot have you in my shop every day mooning over what you have lost."

"Yes sir," said Bryce.

Lucius sighed again. He got up from his work-bench and went to Edward's shelf and picked him up and held him so that Bryce could see him.

"Hey, Jangles," said Bryce. "You look good. The last time I seen you, you looked terrible, your head was busted in and—"

"He is put together again," said Lucius, "as I promised you he would be."

Bryce nodded. He wiped his hand across his nose.

"Can I hold him?" he asked.

"No," said Lucius.

Bryce nodded again.

"Tell him goodbye," said Lucius Clarke. "He is repaired. He has been saved. Now you must tell him goodbye."

"Goodbye," said Bryce.

Don't go, thought Edward. I won't be able to bear it if you go.

"And now you must leave," said Lucius Clarke.

"Yes, sir," said Bryce. But he stood without moving, looking at Edward.

"Go," said Lucius Clarke, "go."

Please, thought Edward, don't.

Bryce turned. He walked through the door of the doll mender's shop. The door closed. The bell tinkled.

And Edward was alone.

CHAPTER TWENTY-FIVE

TECHNICALLY, OF COURSE, HE WAS not alone. Lucius Clarke's shop was filled with dolls—lady dolls and baby dolls, dolls with eyes that opened and closed and dolls with painted-on eyes, dolls dressed as queens and dolls wearing sailor suits.

Edward had never cared for dolls. He found them annoying and self-centered, twittery and vain. This opinion was immediately reinforced by his first shelf-mate, a china doll with green glass eyes and red lips and dark brown hair. She was wearing a green satin dress that fell to her knees.

"What are *you?*" she said in a high-pitched voice when Edward was placed on the shelf next to her.

"I am a rabbit," said Edward.

The doll let out a small squeak. "You're in the wrong place," she said. "This is a shop for dolls. Not rabbits."

Edward said nothing.

"Shoo," said the doll.

"I would love to shoo," said Edward, "but it is obvious that I cannot."

After a long silence, the doll said, "I hope you don't think that anyone is going to buy you."

Again, Edward said nothing.

"The people who come in here want dolls, not rabbits. They want baby dolls or elegant dolls such as myself, dolls with pretty dresses, dolls with eyes that open and close."

"I have no interest in being purchased," said Edward.

The doll gasped. "You don't want somebody to buy you?" she said. "You don't want to be owned by a little girl who loves you?"

Sarah Ruth! Abilene! Their names went through Edward's head like the notes of a sad, sweet song.

"I have already been loved," said Edward. "I have been loved by a girl named Abilene. I have been loved by a fisherman and his wife and a hobo and his dog. I have been loved by a boy who played the harmonica and by a girl who died. Don't talk to me about love," he said. "I have known love."

This impassioned speech shut up Edward's shelf-mate for a considerable amount of time.

"Well," she said at last, "still. My point is that no one is going to buy you."

They did not speak to each other again. The doll was sold two weeks later to a grandmother who was purchasing her for a grandchild. "Yes," she said to Lucius Clarke, "that one right there, the one with the green dress. She is quite lovely."

"Yes," said Lucius, "she is, isn't she?" And he plucked the doll from the shelf.

Goodbye and good riddance, thought Edward.

The spot next to the rabbit stayed vacant for some time. Day after day, the door to the shop opened and closed, letting in early morning sun or late afternoon light, lifting the hearts of the dolls inside, all of them thinking when the door swung wide that this time, this time, the person entering the shop would be the one who wanted them.

Edward was the lone contrarian. He prided himself on not hoping, on not allowing his heart to lift inside of him. He prided himself on keeping his heart silent, immobile, closed tight.

I am done with hope, thought Edward Tulane.

And then one day at dusk, right before he closed the shop, Lucius Clarke placed another doll on the shelf next to Edward.

CHAPTER TWENTY-SIX

THERE YOU ARE, MILADY. MEET THE rabbit doll," said Lucius.

The doll mender walked away, turning out the lights one by one.

In the gloom of the shop, Edward could see that the doll's head, like his, had been broken and repaired. Her face was, in fact, a web of cracks. She was wearing a baby bonnet.

"How do you do?" she said in a high, thin voice. "I am pleased to make your acquaintance."

"Hello," said Edward.

"Have you been here long?" she asked.

"Months and months," said Edward. "But I don't care. One place is the same as another to me."

"Oh, not for me," said the doll. "I have lived one hundred years. And in that time, I have been in places that were heavenly and others that were horrid. After a time, you learn that each place is different. And you become a different doll in each place, too. Quite different."

"One hundred years?" said Edward.

"I am old. The doll mender confirmed this. He said as he was mending me that I am at least that. At least one hundred. At least one hundred years old."

Edward thought about everything that had happened to him in his short life. What kind of adventures would you have if you were in the world for a century?

The old doll said, "I wonder who will come for me this time. Someone will come. Someone always comes. Who will it be?"

"I don't care if anyone comes for me," said Edward.

"But that's dreadful," said the old doll. "There's no point in going on if you feel that way. No point at all. You must be filled with expectancy. You must be awash in hope. You must wonder who will love you, whom you will love next."

"I am done with being loved," Edward told her. "I'm done with loving. It's too painful."

"Pish," said the old doll. "Where is your courage?"

"Somewhere else, I guess," said Edward.

"You disappoint me," she said. "You disappoint me greatly. If you have no intention of loving or being loved, then the whole journey is pointless. You might as well leap from this shelf right now and let yourself shatter into a million pieces. Get it over with. Get it all over with now."

"I would leap if I was able," said Edward.

"Shall I push you?" said the old doll.

"No, thank you," Edward said to her. "Not that you could," he muttered to himself.

"What's that?"

"Nothing," said Edward.

The dark in the doll shop was now complete. The old doll and Edward sat on their shelf and stared straight ahead.

"You disappoint me," said the old doll.

Her words made Edward think of Pellegrina: of warthogs and princesses, of listening and love, of spells and curses. What if there *was* somebody waiting to love him? What if there was somebody whom he would love again? Was it possible?

Edward felt his heart stir.

No, he told his heart. Not possible. Not possible.

In the morning, Lucius Clarke came and unlocked the shop, "Good morning, my darlings," he called out to them. "Good morning, my lovelies." He pulled up the shades on the windows. He turned on the light over his tools. He switched the sign on the door to OPEN.

The first customer was a little girl with her father.

"Are you looking for something special?" Lucius Clarke said to them.

"Yes," said the girl, "I am looking for a friend."

Her father put her on his shoulders and they walked slowly around the shop. The girl studied each doll carefully. She looked Edward right in the eyes. She nodded at him.

"Have you decided, Natalie?" her father asked.

"Yes," she said, "I want the one in the baby bonnet."

"Oh," said Lucius Clarke, "you know that she is very old. She is an antique."

"She needs me," said Natalie firmly.

Next to Edward, the old doll let out a sigh. She seemed to sit up straighter. Lucius came and took her off the shelf and handed her to Natalie. And when they left, when the girl's father opened the door for his daughter and the old doll, a bright

EDWARD'S HEART STIRRED.

shaft of early morning light came flooding in, and Edward heard quite clearly, as if she were still sitting next to him, the old doll's voice.

"Open your heart," she said gently. "Someone will come. Someone will come for you. But first you must open your heart."

The door closed. The sunlight disappeared.

Someone will come.

Edward's heart stirred. He thought, for the first time in a long time, of the house on Egypt Street and of Abilene winding his watch and then bending toward him and placing it on his left leg, saying: I will come home to you.

No, no, he told himself. Don't believe it. Don't let yourself believe it.

But it was too late.

Someone will come for you.

The china rabbit's heart had begun, again, to open.

CHAPTER TWENTY-SEVEN

Seasons passed, fall and winter and spring and summer. Leaves blew in through the open door of Lucius Clarke's shop, and rain, and the green outrageous hopeful light of spring. People came and went, grandmothers and doll collectors and little girls with their mothers.

Edward Tulane waited.

The seasons turned into years.

Edward Tulane waited.

He repeated the old doll's words over and over until they wore a smooth groove of hope in his brain: *Someone will come; someone will come for you.*

And the old doll was right.

Someone did come.

It was springtime. It was raining. There were dogwood blossoms on the floor of Lucius Clarke's shop.

She was a small girl, maybe five years old, and while her mother struggled to close a blue umbrella, the little girl walked around the store, stopping and staring solemnly at each doll and then moving on.

When she came to Edward, she stood in front of him for what seemed like a long time. She looked at him and he looked back at her.

Someone will come, Edward said. *Someone will come for me.*

The girl smiled and then she stood on her tip-toes and took Edward off the shelf. She cradled him in her arms. She held him in the same ferocious, tender way Sarah Ruth had held him.

Oh, thought Edward, I remember this.

"Madam," said Lucius Clarke, "could you please attend to your daughter. She is holding a very fragile, very precious, quite expensive doll."

"Maggie," said the woman. She looked up from the still-open umbrella. "What have you got?"

"A rabbit," said Maggie.

"A what?" said the mother.

"A rabbit," said Maggie again. "I want him."

"Remember, we're not buying anything today. We're looking only," said the woman.

"Madam," said Lucius Clarke, "please."

The woman came and stood over Maggie. She looked down at Edward.

The rabbit felt dizzy.

He wondered, for a minute, if his head had cracked open again, if he was dreaming.

"Look, Mama," said Maggie, "look at him."

"I see him," said the woman.

She dropped the umbrella. She put her hand

on the locket that hung around her neck. And Edward saw then that it was not a locket at all. It was a watch, a pocket watch.

It was his watch.

"Edward?" said Abilene.

Yes, said Edward.

"Edward," she said again, certain this time.

Yes, said Edward, yes, yes, yes.

It's me.

CODA

ONCE, THERE WAS A CHINA RABBIT WHO was loved by a little girl. The rabbit went on an ocean journey and fell overboard and was rescued by a fisherman. He was buried under garbage and unburied by a dog. He traveled for a long time with the hoboes and worked for a short time as a scarecrow.

Once, there was a rabbit who loved a little girl and watched her die.

The rabbit danced on the streets of Memphis. His head was broken open in a diner and was put together again by a doll mender.

And the rabbit swore that he would not make the mistake of loving again.

Once there was a rabbit who danced in a garden in springtime with the daughter of the woman who had loved him at the beginning of his journey. The girl swung the rabbit as she danced in circles. Sometimes, they went so fast, the two of them, that it seemed as if they were flying. Sometimes, it seemed as if they both had wings.

Once, oh marvelous once, there was a rabbit who found his way home.

Questions to Consider

1. The day the maid misplaces Edward, Abilene runs from room to room, calling for him. Why does Abilene love him so much? What emotion does Edward feel in return and why?

2. Why does Pellegrina tell the story to Abilene and Edward about a princess who loves no one and is turned into a warthog by a witch?

3. How does Lolly feel when she discovers that her parents are treating Edward like a "rabbit child" (page 79)? What do you think of her decision to get rid of Edward?

4. Bull describes himself and Lucy as "lost" (page 92). What does he mean by that?

5. When the old woman uses Edward as a scarecrow, he feels mocked by the stars, which seem to say, "You are down there alone." When he tells the stars, "I have been loved," they reply, "What difference does that make when you are all alone now?" (pages 119–120). What do you think? Does being loved change the way loneliness is felt?

6. In the doll store, Edward "prided himself on not hoping, on not allowing his heart to lift inside of him. He prided himself on keeping his heart silent, immobile, closed tight. I am done with hope, thought Edward Tulane" (page 194). Why does Edward feel this way? Do you think this is the right decision?

ONE COMMUNITY

ONE SCHOOL

ONE BOOK

When an entire community reads the same book, it becomes a point of reference for all members of that community. Conversation is sparked between booksellers and customers, librarians and patrons, teachers and students, parents and children, neighbors and friends. Reading becomes a part of that conversation. Kate DiCamillo began championing community reads initiatives across the country during her tenure as National Ambassador for Young People's Literature, and she has seen firsthand the profound impact of shared reading experiences with her own books.

For discussion guides and other resources
for Kate DiCamillo's books, please visit
WWW.KATEDICAMILLOSTORIESCONNECTUS.COM.

Join in the conversation online using #KateDiCamillo.

Follow Kate DiCamillo on Facebook at
FACEBOOK.COM/KATEDICAMILLO.

Louisiana Elefante doesn't
want to leave
her home and her family,
but she seems destined
only for good-byes.

When Granny wakes her up in the middle of the
night to tell her that the day of reckoning has
arrived and they have to leave home immediately,
Louisiana isn't overly worried. After all, Granny
has many middle-of-the-night ideas. But this
time, things are different. This time, Granny
intends for them never to return.

Turn the page for an excerpt . . .

A #1 New York Times Bestseller

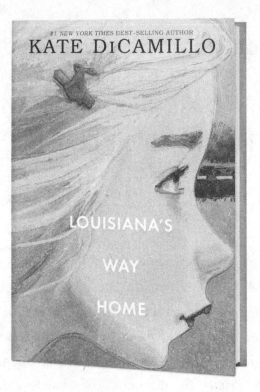

★ "A special treat." — *Kirkus Reviews* (starred review)

★ "Beautiful [and] bittersweet." — *Shelf Awareness* (starred review)

"Louisiana . . . operates with a sense of wonder and practical optimism (the pages shine with it)." — *The New York Times Book Review*

This is what happened.

We stood on the side of the road.

In Georgia.

Just past the Florida-Georgia state line. Which is not at all—in any way—a line. Yet people insist that it exists. Think about that.

Granny turned to me and said, "All will be well."

I said, "I do not believe you."

I refused to look at her.

We were both quiet for a very long time.

an excerpt from LOUISIANA'S WAY HOME

Three semis drove past us. One was painted with a picture of a cow standing in a field of green grass. I was jealous of that cow because she was at home and I was not.

It seemed like a very sad thing to be jealous of a fake cow on the side of a truck.

I must warn you that a great deal of this story is extremely sad.

When the third semi blew past us without even slowing down, Granny said, "I am only attending to your best interests."

Well, what was in my best interests was being with Raymie Clarke and Beverly Tapinski. Raymie and Beverly were the friends of my heart, and they had been my best friends for two solid years. I could not survive without them. I couldn't. It was just not possible.

So what I said to Granny was, "I want to go home. Being with Archie is in my best interests. Raymie and Beverly and Buddy the one-eyed

dog are in my best interests. You don't understand anything about my best interests."

"Now is not the time," said Granny. "This
conversation is inopportune. I feel extremely
unwell. But nonetheless, I am persevering. As
should you."

Well, I did not care that Granny felt extremely
unwell.

And I was tired of persevering.

I crossed my arms over my chest. I stared
down at the ground. There were a lot of ants
running around on the side of the highway
looking very busy and pleased with themselves.
Why would ants choose to live on the side of a
highway where they were just going to get run
over by cars and semis on a regular basis?

Since I was not talking to Granny, there was
no one in the world for me to ask this question of.

It was a very lonely feeling.

And then an old man in a pickup truck
stopped.

. . .

The old man in the pickup truck was named George LaTrell.

He rolled down his window and raised his cap off his head and said, "Howdy, I am George LaTrell."

I smiled at him.

It is best to smile. That is what Granny has told me my whole life. If you have to choose between smiling and not smiling, choose smiling. It fools people for a short time. It gives you an advantage.

According to Granny.

"Now, what are you two lovely ladies doing on the side of the road?" said George LaTrell.

"Good morning, George LaTrell," said Granny. "It seems we have miscalculated and run entirely out of gasoline." She smiled a very large smile. She used all of her teeth.

"Miscalculated," said George LaTrell. "Run entirely out of gasoline. My gracious."

an excerpt from LOUISIANA'S WAY HOME

"Could we impose upon you for a ride to the nearest gas station and back again?" said Granny.

"You could impose upon me," said George LaTrell.

I considered not imposing upon George LaTrell, because the truth is that in addition to being tired of persevering, I was also tired of imposing. Granny and I were always imposing on people. That is how we got by. We imposed. Also, we borrowed.

Sometimes we stole.

I considered not getting into the truck. I considered running down the highway, back to Florida.

But I did not think I would be able to run fast enough.

I have never been able to run fast enough.

And by that I mean that no matter where I go, Granny seems to find me.

Is that fate? Destiny? The power of Granny?

I do not know.

I got in the truck.

an excerpt from LOUISIANA'S WAY HOME

. . .

The inside of George LaTrell's truck smelled like tobacco and vinyl. The seat was ripped up, and stuffing was coming out of it in places.

"We certainly do appreciate this, George LaTrell," said Granny.

Once somebody told Granny what their name was, she never lost a chance to use it. She said that people liked to hear the sound of their own names above and beyond any other sound in the world. She said it was a scientifically proven fact.

I doubted it very sincerely.

I sat in George LaTrell's truck and picked at the stuffing coming out of the seat, and then I threw the little pieces of stuffing fluff out the window.

"Stop that, Louisiana," said Granny.

But I didn't stop.

I threw pieces of truck stuffing out the window, and I thought about the people (and animals) I had left behind.

an excerpt from LOUISIANA'S WAY HOME

Raymie Clarke, who loved to read and who listened to all of my stories.

Beverly Tapinski, who was afraid of nothing and who was very good at picking locks.

And then there was Archie, who was King of the Cats.

And Buddy the one-eyed dog, who was also known to us as the Dog of Our Hearts.

What if I never got the chance to use those names again?

What if I was destined to never again stand in front of those people (and that cat and that dog) and say their names out loud to them?

It was a tragic thought.

I threw more stuffing from George LaTrell's truck window. The stuffing looked like snow flying through the air. If you squinted, it did. If you squinted really hard.

I am good at squinting.

. . .

an excerpt from LOUISIANA'S WAY HOME

George LaTrell took us to a gas station called Vic's Value. Granny started the work of talking Mr. LaTrell into pumping some gas into a can for her and also making him pay for what he pumped.

And since I had no desire to witness her efforts to get the gas that would only take me farther from my home and friends, I walked away from the two of them and went inside Vic's Value, where it smelled like motor oil and dirt. There was a tall counter with a cash register on it.

Next to the cash register, there was a rack that was full of bags of salted peanuts, and even though my heart was broken and I was filled with the most terrible despair, my goodness, I was hungry.

I stared very hard at those little bags of peanuts.

The man behind the counter was sitting on a chair that had wheels, and when he saw me, he came out from behind the counter like a spider, moving his feet back and forth and back and forth. The chair made a squeaky exasperated noise as it rolled toward me.

"How do you do?" I said. I smiled, using all of my teeth. "My granny is outside getting some gas."

The man turned his head and looked at Granny and George LaTrell, and then he looked back at me.

"Yep," he said.

I considered him.

He had a lot of hair in his nose.

"How much are your peanuts?" I said.

I said this even though I did not have any money at all. Granny always said, "Ask the price exactly as if you intend to pay."

The man didn't answer me.

"Are you Vic?" I said.

"Could be."

"I am Louisiana Elefante."

"Yep," he said.

He took a yellow spotted handkerchief out of

his pocket and wiped it across his forehead. His hands were almost entirely black with grease.

I said, "I have been made to leave home against my will."

"That right there is the story of the world," said Vic.

"It is?" I said.

"Yep."

"I hate it," I said. "I have friends at home."

Vic nodded. He folded his spotted handkerchief up into a neat square and put it back in his pocket.

"You can take as many of them little bags of peanuts as you want to," he said. He nodded in the direction of the peanut rack.

"Free of charge," he said. And then he rolled himself back around the counter.

Well, this was the only good thing that had happened to me since Granny woke me up at three a.m. and told me that the day of reckoning had arrived.

In some ways, this is a story of woe and

an excerpt from LOUISIANA'S WAY HOME

confusion, but it is also a story of joy and kindness and free peanuts.

"Thank you," I said.

I helped myself to fourteen bags.

Vic smiled at me the whole time I was taking the peanuts from the rack.

There is goodness in many hearts.

In most hearts.

In some hearts.

I love peanuts.

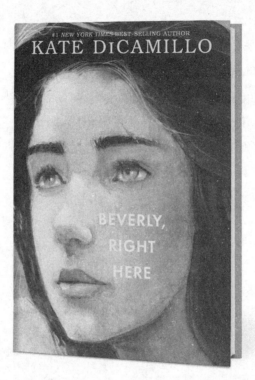

★ "Deeply meaningful." —*Publishers Weekly* (starred review)

★ "DiCamillo writes in a spare style, describing small, seemingly disparate moments that gradually come together in a rich, dynamic picture. The other thing she does brilliantly is shape characters whose eccentricities make them heartbreakingly, vividly real." —*Booklist* (starred review)

Beverly Tapinski has
run away from home
plenty of times,
but that was when
she was just a kid.

This time, it's not running away. It's leaving. She tries
to forget about her dog, now buried underneath the
orange trees back home; her friend, whom she left
without a word; and her mom, who has never cared
about anyone but herself. Beverly doesn't want to
depend on anyone, and she definitely doesn't want
anyone to depend on her. But despite her best efforts,
she can't help forming connections with the people
around her—and gradually, she learns to see herself
through their eyes.

More from Kate DiCamillo

A Newbery
Honor Book

A National Book
Award Finalist

Winner of the
Newbery Medal

A *New York
Times* Bestseller

Winner of the
Newbery Medal

A National Book
Award Finalist